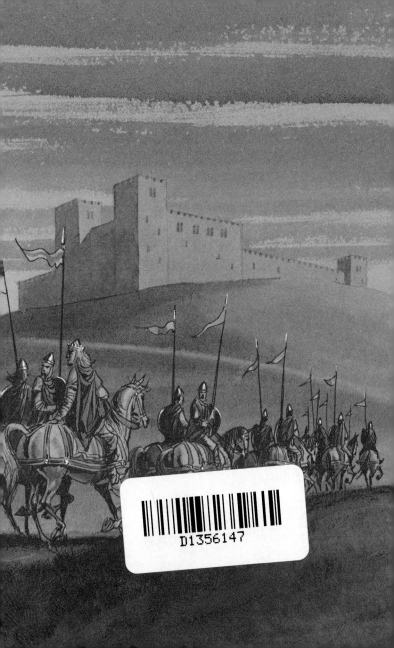

The legend of King Arthur has come down to us out of the dim mists of history. All we know for certain is that when the Romans left Britain a warrior chief led a band of brave followers against the Saxon invaders. Around his heroic deeds grew the legend of Arthur and Excalibur, of Merlin and the Knights of the Round Table.

Like all good legends it has grown with the telling and who is to say that so brave a company would not also have found time to undertake adventurous deeds on behalf of the weak, the poor and the oppressed?

These are some of the stories from the legend. They may not have happened at all—but we can hope they did.

A certain amount of artist's licence has been found necessary in preparing the illustrations, in view of the lack of precise information about the period.

The knight of the
golden falcon

by DESMOND DUNKERLEY

with illustrations by
ROBERT AYTON

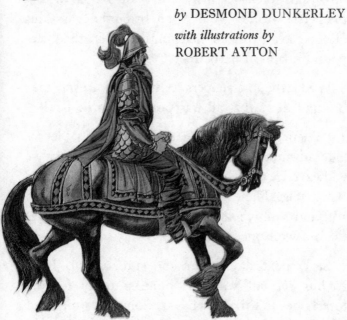

Ladybird Books Ltd Loughborough 1977

THE KNIGHT OF THE GOLDEN FALCON

The winter had been cold and hard. Few of King Arthur's court had ridden far from Camelot during the long dark months, but now spring though late had come at last. With it came thoughts of action and adventure. As soon as the last of the snow had disappeared the king sent messengers out in all directions for news of his kingdom. He knew that the better weather would again bring the long ships of the Saxon pirates, held until now in their ice-bound northern harbours.

When the messengers returned however they brought news that all was peaceful in the land.

"Then," said the king to his Council, "let us take advantage of this quiet time. Tomorrow we will exercise ourselves and our horses and hunt the forest stag. Then will our arms and legs be not so stiff and sore when the time comes for us to hunt the sea wolf once again!"

Early next day before the sun was up King Arthur set out with his hunting party for the forests beyond the River Usk. Soon after they had left, Queen Guinevere thought that she too would enjoy the fresh air and the sunshine. So with but one of her ladies to keep her company, the queen rode to the top of a hill overlooking the river.

"We will wait here and
watch the hunt," she said, "for it is
warm and, see, we can look around for miles."

Suddenly they heard the sound of hooves, and a
tall young man rode out of the trees towards them.
He was not in armour, nor was he dressed for
hunting. He wore court clothes, his only weapon a
light, gold-handled sword.

5

The rider bowed low to Queen Guinevere, who greeted him gaily.

"You are most welcome, Sir Geraint," she said. "But why are you not hunting with the king?"

"He had gone, my lady, before I knew of it," replied the young knight, "but when I was told that you had gone out alone without protection I came to offer mine."

"We welcome both your protection and your company," said the queen. "See, the hunt should pass below there quite soon."

While they stood talking they heard amongst the trees the clank of armour and the trample of horses. They looked round to see a knight in full armour, mounted on a great war-horse, riding past them, followed by a richly dressed lady on a pure white horse with gold and silver harness. Behind her rode a little dark man with a fierce and bearded face. On the dwarf's back hung the knight's shield. In his left hand he carried his master's lance, while from his right hung a long, knotted whip. The three passed by without a sideways glance.

"Who is that warlike knight?" the queen asked.

"I know not, lady, for his face was covered by his helmet and his shield was also hidden," replied Geraint, "but I will go and ask his page." He rode up to the dwarf. "The queen would know your master's name," he said.

"I will not tell you," replied the dwarf rudely.

"Then I will ask him myself," said Geraint.

"That you will not," said the fierce little man, "for you are not a noble enough knight to speak to him," and as Geraint turned his horse's head the dwarf lashed out with his whip. The knotted lash caught Geraint across the mouth. Angrily the young knight began to draw his sword.

Then Geraint realised that if he killed the dwarf he would immediately be attacked by the knight, who had stopped at the sound of the raised voices. Since he had but a light sword, Geraint knew that he would be no match for the fully armed knight. He thrust his sword back into its scabbard and returned to the queen.

"I am sorry you suffered that insult for my sake, sir," she said gently. Geraint's face was calm, but his eyes were angry as he bowed to Queen Guinevere.

"An insult I would avenge, your majesty," he said quietly. "So with your permission I will follow them until I can obtain arms and armour. Then will I know that proud knight's name."

"We shall wait anxiously for word that you have done so and are safe," said Guinevere. "God go with you."

All that day Geraint followed the unknown knight, the lady and the dwarf, never allowing himself to be seen but always keeping them in sight.

At length, as the sun was beginning to set, they rode into a small town beside the grey walls of a tall castle. As the proud knight rode through the streets the people by the wayside bowed to him with great respect, but he did not even turn his head to left or right to return their greetings.

Once Geraint had seen them enter the castle and knew that they would stay there, he set about looking for someone he knew with whom he could lodge and from whom he could borrow arms and armour. But although the narrow streets were full of knights and squires and their armour-bearers, cleaning armour, sharpening swords and lance points, Geraint saw no face he recognised.

Right through the town he rode and crossed the stream which ran by the outer wall. There he came upon an old manor house with tumbledown walls and grass and weeds growing high in the courtyard.

Thinking the house deserted, Geraint was about to search elsewhere when an old man, dressed in clothes that had once been rich, came up to him.

"Is there any way, young sir, that I can help you?" he asked.

"I seek a night's lodgings, sir," replied Geraint, "for I have ridden far."

"Then you are welcome here," said the old man. "We have not much to offer, but what we have we will gladly share with you."

He led Geraint into the house to where an old woman sat. Her clothes, also, were old and tattered, but Geraint saw at once that they too had once been fine and of good material.

"Please join us, sir, in the meal my daughter Enid is preparing," said the old lady as a girl entered the hall with a platter of meat and bread.

Sir Geraint thought that he had never in his life seen a lovelier maiden, even though her face was pale and her clothes were thin and old like those of her parents.

After they had eaten, Geraint asked to whom the old manor house belonged.

"To me," said the old man sadly, "as did once the castle up there, and all the lands nearby."

"Then how did you come to lose so much?" asked Geraint in great astonishment.

"By my own greed," answered the old man slowly. "I am Earl Liconyl but an earl in name only now. I have a nephew whom I cared for when his father, my brother, died. I was to look after his lands until he himself was old enough. But I took them for myself and added them to my own. Then, when the boy became a man he demanded back his lands and I, in my greed and foolishness, would not return them."

"So he took them all – and left you this?" said Geraint, and the old man nodded his head with a sigh.

Geraint was silent for a moment.

"Since you now regret your deeds," he said at length, "I will do all I can to regain for you what you have lost. But tell me," Geraint continued, "about the proud knight who, with his lady and a dwarfish page, stays now at the castle. And why are armourers so busy in the streets?"

"The preparations are for tomorrow's tournament," replied the old earl, "the prize for which is a Falcon of pure gold. The knight you speak of has won the Falcon for the past two years and if, tomorrow, he wins it for a third time then it becomes his own. Each year he stays at the castle with the young earl, my nephew, who likes him not but dares not refuse him."

"I like not this proud knight either, and have a score to settle with him," said Geraint. "Through his dwarf he did insult the fair queen of my lord, King Arthur, so I would joust with him tomorrow had I but arms and armour."

"I have armour here that you may have and gladly," said the Earl Liconyl, "but for tomorrow's tournament your needs are more than that. No knight may challenge for the Falcon trophy," he explained, "unless he does so for the lady of his choice, who must go with him to the lists."

"Then, sir," replied Geraint, "with your permission, and if your daughter would have it so, I will tomorrow make the challenge in her name."

The earl at once agreed, and the Lady Enid's pale face flushed as she gently nodded her head, for she had never seen a nobler or more handsome knight than Geraint.

The next morning was clear and bright, the spring sunshine reflecting on the pure gold Falcon set on its stand before the seat of the young earl. A trumpet signalled for the first challenge and immediately the proud knight rode out with his lady.

"Fetch me the Golden Falcon," he called to her in a deep voice, "for I claim you are the fairest lady on earth." The lady was about to ride forward when Geraint cried, "Touch not the Falcon yet, for I, too, claim it, for the Lady Enid!"

As Geraint rode out onto the field all the spectators laughed, for he wore an old and rusty suit of armour of a style long since out of fashion. The shield he carried was also rusty and bore no design so that none there knew who he was.

But when the two knights had crashed together fiercely several times and each time broken their lances, the people began to wonder who this knight in the rusty armour could be. Then the old Earl Liconyl went up to Geraint saying, "Noble sir, since other lances seem not strong enough, take this one which I was given when I received my knighthood."

Again the two knights crashed together and a great roar rose from the crowd, for this time only the proud knight's lance shattered and he himself was flung to the ground. Geraint leapt from his horse and drew his sword. The fallen knight rose quickly to his feet and they fought fiercely and long,

each dealing the other many hard and wounding blows. But whereas his opponent seemed gradually to tire, Geraint remembered both the insult to Queen Guinevere and the beauty of the Lady Enid, and fought even more strongly.

At last Geraint managed so great a blow that the proud knight was knocked to his knees.

"Mercy!" cried the fallen knight breathlessly. "Spare my life, I beg you!"

18

"Why should I spare the life of a knight so proud that he insults the queen?" asked Geraint coldly.

"I admit my fault, sir, and much regret it," said the fallen knight. "Spare my life and I will change my ways."

"Go then to Queen Guinevere at Camelot. Admit your fault and make that promise to her. Tell her that Geraint of Cornwall sent you."

As none of the other knights there would challenge so fierce and famous a fighter, Sir Geraint was presented with the Golden Falcon by the young earl who then invited him to the castle.

"That I will not," replied Sir Geraint in a stern voice. "I will go back to the old manor house."

When he arrived there with the Earl Liconyl and the Lady Enid they found, to their astonishment, that the young earl had sent his servants before them to clean the house and prepare a great feast in Geraint's honour. The young earl himself was there to meet them.

"Dear uncle," he said, kneeling at the old earl's feet, "may I now, before this most noble Knight of the Round Table, return to you all that is yours by right and ask forgiveness."

Then there was great rejoicing and the feast was a most happy one. As it neared its end Geraint rose to his feet and all were silent.

"My lord Earl," he said, "I believe it is the custom for the new Knight of the Golden Falcon to ask for two favours. These, then, are mine. First, I ask that I may keep the suit of old armour that I borrowed from you for today's jousting. Rusty it may be but it served me well and I would keep it to remind me of this day."

There was laughter and applause as Earl Liconyl smiled and nodded his head.

"Secondly, my lord," went on Geraint, "I ask for the greatest gift a father can give – the hand of your daughter, Enid, if she will have it so, for I do truly love her and would take her with me to Camelot and marry her."

There was great excitement as the old earl rose to his feet. His daughter's happy face gave her answer, so he took her hand and placed it in that of Sir Geraint, the Knight of the Golden Falcon.

THE WAGER OF
SIR BALIN AND SIR BORS

"This is the most shameful message that I have ever received," said King Arthur angrily to the two messengers who knelt before him. "Return now to your King Ryons with this reply. Tell him that I refuse his insolent demands and warn him, further, that if he leaves his kingdom of North Wales and tries to take the land he claims of me by force, then I shall ride against him with all my knights and crush him utterly."

Even as King Ryons' men departed messengers were riding out far and wide to summon the Knights of the Round Table to attend a Council at Camelot, for King Arthur knew that he could not trust the Welsh king. He must prepare for war and it would take many days for his knights to assemble.

Two of the first to answer the summons were Sir Balin and Sir Bors, twin sons of a king of Cornwall. They were among the youngest of King

Arthur's knights and although already famous for their skill at swordplay and jousting, they had yet to prove themselves in war or some great adventure.

Now the brothers were together in the great hall, away from the other knights, arguing in friendly fashion.

"I do not know what venture this is that our lord the king needs to summon all his knights," said Bors, "for I have no doubt that it is one that I could manage alone!"

Balin smiled. "If it were an adventure requiring one lance only," he replied, "the king would hardly look to you, or even Lancelot himself, whilst I am here."

"You place yourself with Lancelot?" laughed Bors. "It's fortunate for you he is not here to listen to the boast."

"A wager, then!" cried Balin gaily, clapping his hand on his brother's shoulder. "Whatever task or adventure arises from this Council of the king, I will complete it first and prove I am the stronger knight and the fiercer fighter!"

"Agreed!" said Bors, clasping the other's hand. "But see, the king and his war council come, and never have I seen them look in such a rage."

The knights took their places at the Round Table and listened in angry silence as King Arthur told them of King Ryons' threats.

"This is no task for one lance, brother, even mine," whispered Bors to Balin, "for this Ryons is said to be a fierce warrior and to command many men as warlike as himself."

"I have heard it is so," replied Balin. "Our wager had perhaps best wait until a happier time."

At that moment the doors of the great hall swung open and a young maiden entered.

"Most noble lord, King Arthur," she said, standing before the king, "I bring a message from King Ryons of North Wales through whose lands I have just passed." All there fell silent waiting for the lady to continue. "He bids me say that since you will not give, then he will take."

The knights again began to talk fiercely and seeing, too, how the king's face had darkened at her words, the maiden added hastily, "I know not what the message means, my lord, and only speak as I was bidden. So now, with your leave, I will depart again upon my quest."

She turned to go, but King Arthur called her back, silencing his angry knights with a wave of the hand.

"Stay, lady, stay," he said gently, "for you must know that our anger was not meant for you, but only for the false king whose words you carried. Besides," the king continued, "we all would know more of this quest you spoke of, which brought you through North Wales to Camelot."

"This then, my lord," the maiden replied, throwing back her cloak to reveal a great sword in a scabbard fastened to her belt.

"Why do you wear that?" asked Arthur in astonishment.

"It is a penance, sir," she said, "and my quest is for a true and blameless knight, for only such a one can draw this sword from its scabbard and rid me of its burden. None at King Ryons' court could do it," she continued, "and I hoped to find one here to help me. But then I made you angry and dared not ask."

"A great marvel indeed," said King Arthur, "although I am not surprised that you failed to find the knight you seek among Ryons' followers. So now let me try, and if I fail one of my knights will surely be the one to free you from your penance." So saying the king grasped the scabbard firmly in one hand and the sword hilt in the other. But pull as he might, the sword would not move.

"No strength is needed, lord," the maiden said, "for the right man's hand will free it easily."

Then one by one all tried without success to draw the sword until only Sir Balin and Sir Bors remained, for being youngest they had waited until the last. Sir Bors tried first and the sword stayed fast. As Sir Balin stepped forward all were silent, half hoping that the young knight would not succeed where they had failed. There was a murmur of amazement as the sword slid softly into Balin's hand.

"Nobly done!" cried King Arthur, well pleased that one of his Round Table had done what none at the hated Ryons' court had managed.

"Nobly done, indeed, my lord," said the maiden. Then turning to Sir Balin she said, "Now, gentle sir, I beg you give me back my sword so that I may destroy it."

"Give it back?" cried Balin in amazement. "Never! The sword is mine now."

"You are not wise to keep it," said the maiden sadly, "for with it you will kill your best friend and the man in the world you hold most dear."

But Balin remained firm and so the maiden departed in great sorrow, while King Arthur continued his interrupted Council.

Balin and Bors, however, did not stay. They were determined to wait no longer for the great adventure which would prove their knighthood, but instead to go out in search of it. Balin was sure that his new sword would help them with a daring plan which, if successful, would bring them honour and great fame.

"If King Ryons is anything at all of a true knight," he explained excitedly to Bors as they rode, "he will meet our challenge with but one knight to aid him. Then the one of us who kills him will surely be the foremost of King Arthur's knights and our wager will be settled."

"And what if he proves as false as men say he is and sets upon us with all his men?" asked his brother, "or is as fierce a fighter as men say he is and so kills us?"

"Then we shall have died gloriously," replied Balin gaily. "Come, let us ride!" and setting spurs to their horses they galloped off.

*   *   *

In the weeks that followed Camelot was the centre of great warlike preparations and neither King Arthur nor his knights had time to spare for thoughts of Balin and Bors.

Then one morning the sound of cheering in the streets outside brought the king and two of his chief war-leaders, Sir Lancelot and Sir Bedivere, to the battlements of the castle. They looked down in amazement as a file of unarmed knights rode slowly into the courtyard, led by a young knight wearing two swords.

The king hurried below to be met on the steps

by the young knight, who led forward a tall,
bearded warrior clad all in red. The young knight
knelt before the king.

"My lord Arthur," he said, "I, Balin of Cornwall,
bring you as prisoner Ryons of North Wales. My
brother Bors and I defeated him in fair fight and
he is here to pay you homage. With him are fifty
of his knights." Rising to his feet Balin continued,
"Now I will, with your permission, sire, ride again
in search of my brother, for he left to seek
adventures of his own, and a wager between us is
not settled yet."

So saying he rode away leaving King Arthur and
all his court marvelling both at his words and at
the deed he had performed.

In the months that followed Balin had many

strange adventures and became famous far and wide as the Knight with Two Swords. Yet in all that time he heard no word of his brother Bors.

As he continued his search he came one day to a castle where a great feast was prepared in his honour. Afterwards the lord of the castle said, "We have a custom that all who come here must fight with the knight who guards the island yonder."

"It is an evil custom," said Balin quietly, "but I am not afraid to fight."

"Then take this shield," said the lord, "for your own is small and is badly dented from much use."

Taking the new shield and leaving his own behind, Balin crossed the shallow river to the island. There was no moon as yet, and it was difficult to see his way. Suddenly, near at hand, the gates of a castle opened. Light shone forth as a knight in black armour, guarded it seemed by other knights, rode from the castle to meet him. Then darkness descended once more as the gates shut.

Only the glint of sword and armour could be seen as Sir Balin and the black knight, scorning a challenge, clashed together. They fought furiously on horseback and on foot, for more than three hours. At last both fell, mortally wounded.

"Who are you?" said Balin weakly, "for never have I met so brave a knight."

"I am Bors," replied the Black Knight, "brother of the famous knight, Balin."

"Alas, that I should see this day," cried Balin, taking off his helmet. "How come you here? For now we have killed each other."

"Heaven help me," moaned Bors, recognising his brother as the moon rose behind the trees. "I passed this way and killed the knight who guarded

the island. Then I was kept prisoner in his place and forced to fight any who came. It was too dark to recognise you when our fight began."

Balin looked for the last time on the face of the man in the world he held most dear.

"The maiden was right," he whispered.

"And neither of us wins the wager," said Bors softly, grasping the other's hand, "for we were as equal in life as we are in death."

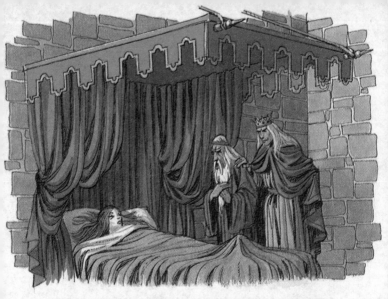

THE KNIGHT OF THE FOUNTAIN

Queen Guinevere lay ill. For two weeks she had not left her bed, and although the first fever had gone the gentle queen seemed unable to regain her strength.

"Is there nothing more you can do, Merlin?" said King Arthur. He paced restlessly up and down as he spoke, for he was sad and worried.

"My strongest herbs and surest remedies do not now seem to help my lady queen at all," replied the old man sadly, shaking his head from side to side. "I know not what else to try, unless . . . " He paused and King Arthur seized his arm eagerly.

"Unless what? Have you thought of something you can do?"

"Not that *I* can do, my lord, although a hundred years ago I would have tried," said Merlin with a little smile. "But this would be a task for a young and valiant knight who is unafraid of danger."

"Then I must go," cried Arthur. "I am young. I have known danger before, and have on occasions past shown valour."

"All those things are true, my lord," said Merlin quietly, "but many knights sit at your Round Table. Bid one of them go, for your place is here with the queen. Besides, the Saxons begin to raid again and soon you may have to lead against them."

"You speak as wisely as I spoke hastily," King Arthur said, "and yet how can I order or even ask one of my faithful knights to face this danger? Guinevere is my wife."

"She is their queen," said Merlin.

"For whom I would gladly face any danger," said a voice behind them gallantly, "without bidding or asking. Just tell me what I must do and where this danger lies, for I heard but the last of your talk as I approached."

Turning round quickly, Arthur grasped the speaker's hand, and greeted him warmly.

"Gawaine," he said, "I do not know yet myself what the danger is, for Merlin has not told me of it. Yet I do know that I cannot let you face it, for you above all I need here at my side."

Gawaine dropped on one knee before the king and pleaded so hard to be allowed to undertake the task that at last King Arthur reluctantly agreed.

So while a squire prepared Sir Gawaine's horse and armour Merlin told them of a mysterious fountain the waters of which were said to cure every kind of illness.

"The fountain is in the courtyard of a strong castle," the old man explained, "which stands in wild forests somewhere far to the north of here."

"I will find it," said Gawaine eagerly.

"Finding it may be the easiest part of your task," said Merlin gravely. "The castle itself is said to be guarded by a fierce knight and the only path to it through the dense forest watched over by a warlike dwarf."

"Then God go with you!" called the king as Gawaine raised his lance in salute and rode away.

At first his way led north along the straight old Roman road through peaceful villages and rich farmlands. But these gradually gave way to wild uncultivated country with little sign of life. Here the road itself, now little used, became grass covered, and finally disappeared altogether. At last he reached a wide river and stood looking across to the opposite bank where dark trees grew thickly down to the water's edge. Shivering slightly Gawaine pulled his cloak closer, for before him lay the vast Northern Forest which stretched all the way to the great Wall itself, built by the Roman emperor Hadrian to keep out the Wild Ones.

Downstream to his right, a stone-built Roman bridge spanned the river. Gawaine rode down to it and saw that although the stonework was crumbling in places it would be possible for him to cross. So he proceeded with caution.

When he reached the gloomy forest on the far side, he saw a small thatched hut hidden in the trees. He knocked on the door with his lance.

"I have nothing to offer you but shelter, my lord," said the old woman who answered his summons. "I have no food."

"Shelter is all I need this night, good woman," replied Gawaine, "and perhaps in the morning some answers to my questions."

He slept soundly on the bed of freshly cut bracken which the old woman had quickly prepared, and woke next morning to the fragrant smell of cooking.

"So great a lord should not ride hungry into the forest," the old woman said, waving with her hand at the trees. "I was up early and found a rabbit in my snare."

"How did you know I was going there?" asked Gawaine, gratefully taking the bowl of food she offered him.

"What other way is there to go from here except back?" replied the old woman.

Gawaine ate in silence for a minute or two, while the old woman sat watching him. Then she asked, "Do you search for the fountain like the others?"

"I do," said Gawaine eagerly. "Can you tell me the way? Of what others do you speak? Did they bring back the waters?"

"So many questions," laughed the old woman. "Yes, I can tell you the way and yes, others have come by here on the same errand. Some went on but as to what they found, that I know not."

"Why is that?" asked Gawaine. "Did they not return this way?"

"There is no other way," replied the old woman, "so those that went on either got lost in the forest, and that's easy enough to do, or were killed by those who guard the fountain. Most of them looked as if they deserved it," she added darkly.

"What of those who turned back?" asked Gawaine.

"They liked not the condition upon which the castle would be unlocked," the woman said.

"Condition?" said Gawaine. "I know of the fierce knight and his warlike dwarf and these I fear not, but what is this condition which unlocks castles, for of this I have not heard?"

The old woman laughed again. "Then I will tell you, my lord," she said. "The Castle of the Fountain belongs to a great lady, but she is kept prisoner there by the fierce knight and his troll. The castle itself is so strongly held that only an army could take it by force. The only way in, even if you conquer those two, is by the key."

"Then where is the key? How do I get it?" demanded Gawaine.

"It is said that the key will be given freely to the Christian knight who first defeats the two guardians of the castle and then swears to marry the lady, even though he must not see her before he makes the promise," replied the old woman.

Gawaine stood up. "That seems a hard condition," he agreed, "for it takes courage to swear to wed an unseen maid. But as I am as yet unwed myself," he laughed, "and as she is no doubt young and beautiful it may not be so hard."

"Not so, my lord," said the old woman, "for it is also said that she is not only ugly but a witch!"

"A witch!" Gawaine cried in horror. "I must promise to marry a witch?"

"It is the only way to the fountain," replied the old woman, "and it is the reason why most of the other searchers go no further."

"But I shall go on nevertheless," said Gawaine, "for in the name of chivalry a knight of the Round Table can leave no lady in captivity if it is within his power to save her. Besides," he added, "my queen is like to die without the healing waters of the fountain."

So with these brave words he armed himself and rode off. The darkness of the forest closed in upon him immediately, and he followed the narrow twisting paths as the old woman had directed.

Towards evening the path, though still narrow, straightened out between high banks on either side. As Gawaine entered this sunken lane he suddenly received so hard a blow on his helmet that he was almost unhorsed. Turning dazedly around he saw a fierce, dark little man above him on the bank, wielding an oaken club. Gawaine thrust at him with his lance, but the troll seized the spear below the point and held it with such strength that Gawaine could not free it. Meanwhile the dwarf was beating at Gawaine with his cudgel, and the blows came so hard and fast that Gawaine's shield was dashed from his grasp.

Suddenly Gawaine spurred his horse forward and the dwarf, still holding the lance, was tumbled from the bank. Letting go his spear and drawing his sword, Gawaine knocked his opponent sense-less to the ground. Then, having picked up his lance and shield, he sat on his horse breathlessly, regaining his strength.

The clank of armour and a shout made Gawaine look up. Ahead of him on the path was a knight in black armour and Gawaine at once levelled his lance and rode at him. Without waiting to fight

the knight wheeled his horse round and rode off at great speed. Greatly surprised at this strange behaviour Gawaine galloped after the black knight, only to see him disappear into a castle, the great door of which slammed shut behind him.

Gawaine rode round the castle walls, angry that because of the black knight's cowardice he would no longer be able to defeat him, which he had to do before the key would be given to him. Then he looked up as a gentle voice called down to him, asking who he was.

"I am Sir Gawaine, a knight of King Arthur's Round Table," he replied, "and I have come to take back to my queen the healing waters of the fountain."

"Ah, Sir Gawaine," answered the voice, "but do you know what must be done and said before that can happen?"

"I know of the conditions, lady," said Gawaine. "The dwarf I have already defeated. The knight, your captor, fled from me but I will gladly fight him if he would but come and face me. As to the last," he went on, "it is hard to wed a lady one has never seen, but no knight of Arthur's company would leave a lady in captivity. So by my knighthood I swear that when I have defeated the coward knight then I will marry you."

"He is no coward," was the strange reply from above, "but now, Gawaine of the Round Table, there is no longer need to fight him."

At these words a large iron key was dropped from the window. Dismounting, Gawaine unlocked the great door and led his horse into the courtyard. His hand dropped quickly to his sword hilt when he saw the knight whom he had chased standing by a splashing fountain. The knight raised his arm in greeting.

"No sword is necessary, noble Gawaine," he said, "for there is no quarrel between us."

"What of the lady you hold prisoner?" demanded Gawaine sternly.

"No prisoner, sir," the other said. "I am Sir Conan and the lady is my dearly loved sister, Elined. Come now and meet her. When you have seen and spoken to her then perhaps you will understand many things."

He led the way to a room where sat the most beautiful maiden Gawaine had ever seen.

He gasped in surprise and the Lady Elined laughed softly.

"No ugly witch, my lord Gawaine," she said, "but a maid who did not wish to marry one of the false adventurers who wanted just my lands and castle, and the fountain."

"We sought a truly brave and chivalrous knight," Sir Conan said, "and now that we have found him we are both agreed we could not hold him to the vow he made. You are free to go, my lord, with such of the fountain's waters as you require."

"I beg you hold me to my vow, fair lady," Gawaine said, kneeling at Elined's feet, "for having seen you I could love no other."

They left for Camelot next day. The waters which they took with them quickly cured Queen Guinevere's illness, and she was able to be present at the wedding of the Lady Elined and Sir Gawaine, her Knight of the Fountain.